Diane Z. Shore · Jessica Alexander

Look Both Ways

A CAUTIONARY TALE

BLOOMSBURY
CHILDREN'S
BOOKS

PICTURES BY Teri Weidner

To Julie,
friend, tennis partner, brochure designer, photographer,
marketer, publicist, banana supplier, babysitter, letter writer,
car driver, diamond painter, dinner maker . . .
Thanks for looking after me in MANY ways. — D. Z. S.

To Julia,
friend to small creatures everywhere.
And to Morgan,
rescuer of same. — J. A.

To Chris Dahlen,
my favorite. — T. W.

Text copyright © 2005 by Diane Z. Shore and Jessica Alexander
Illustrations copyright © 2005 by Teri Weidner
Typeset in Edwardian Medium.
The art was done in pen and ink and watercolor.
Designed by Filomena Tuosto.

Published by Bloomsbury Publishing, New York and London
Distributed to the trade by Holtzbrinck Publishers

Library of Congress Cataloging-in-Publication Data
Shore, Diane ZuHone.
Look both ways : a cautionary tale / by Diane Z. Shore and Jessica Alexander ;
illustrated by Teri Weidner.
   p. cm.
Summary: When Filbert the squirrel goes to his grandmother's to pick up acorns,
he learns the importance of looking both ways before crossing the street.
   ISBN-10: 1-58234-968-1
   ISBN-13: 978-1-58234-968-8
[1. Safety—Fiction. 2. Squirrels—Fiction. 3. Stories in rhyme.]
I. Alexander, Jessica. II. Weidner, Teri, ill. III. Title.
PZ8.3.S55918Lo 2005   [E]—dc22   2004054458

First U.S. Edition 2005
Printed in China
10 9 8 7 6 5 4 3 2 1

Bloomsbury Publishing, Children's Books, U.S.A.
175 Fifth Avenue, New York, NY 10010

All papers used by Bloomsbury Publishing are natural, recyclable products
made from wood grown in well-managed forests. The manufacturing processes
conform to the environmental regulations of the country of origin.

On a crisp, cool day
in a leaf-littered lot,
Filbert kicks the soccer ball
and calls, "My shot!"

Whoosh! down the sideline.
Whizz! through the breeze.
Splat! in the neighbor's
butternut trees.

"Got it!" Filbert runs,
but he's having too much fun
to look . . .
both . . .
ways.

"Nuts!" Mama hollers
in the old oak tree,
counting out acorns,
one, two, three.

"Filbert!" calls Mama
from the back door stoop.
"I need more nuts
for my acorn soup!"

She tosses him a sack.
"Run to Granny's. Hurry back.

And look . . .

both . . .

ways."

Dash! down the drive.
Skip-leap! through the lot.
Filbert tells his friends,
"Back soon! Save my spot!"

Flop! atop the fence.
Hip-hop! along the walk.

Shhh! past the cat
then *zip!* down the block.

He runs across the street,
forgets to stop his feet

and look . . .

both . . .

ways.

Knock, knock! "Who's there?"
Granny peeks past the door.
"Mama's out of nuts.
Can we please have more?"

Granny stuffs the sack.
Filbert stuffs his cheeks.
Granny zips him up
full of honey-nut treats.

She snuggles down his hat.
"Be careful of the cat

and look . . .

both . . .

ways!"

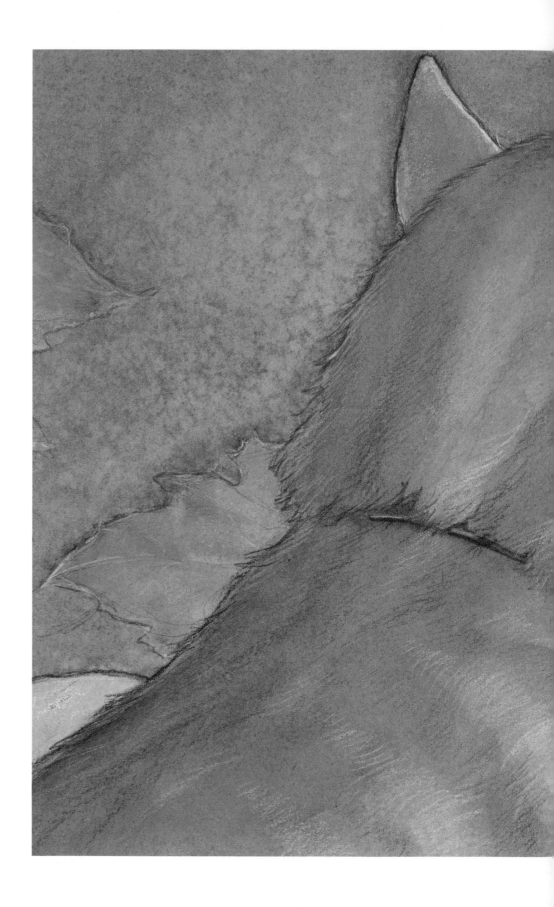

"Thanks, Granny. Love you!"
Filbert hops down the trail.

"MEEEOW!" leaps the cat
zip-zing! on his tail.

Thump! on a rooftop.
Squish! through a hole.
Wiggle-jiggle jump!
down a telephone pole.

He leaves the cat behind
but doesn't see the sign

or look . . .

both . . .

ways.

Cars wheel!

Cars squeal!

Filbert stops and he starts.

Tires turn!
Rubber burns!
Filbert ducks and he darts.

Feet skitter.
Nuts scatter.
Fenders bend.
Horns blare!

Slip-slide!
Clash-clatter!
Nuts fly . . . everywhere!

Filbert scrambles to his feet
as the acorns in the street
all . . .
    roll . . .
        away.

Filbert slumps home.
Sniff-sniff! Boo-hoo!
Mama's at the door.
"What's happened to you?"

"I ran in the street
  and the nuts spilled out."
"Oh, dear." Mama frowns.
"We'll have to do without."

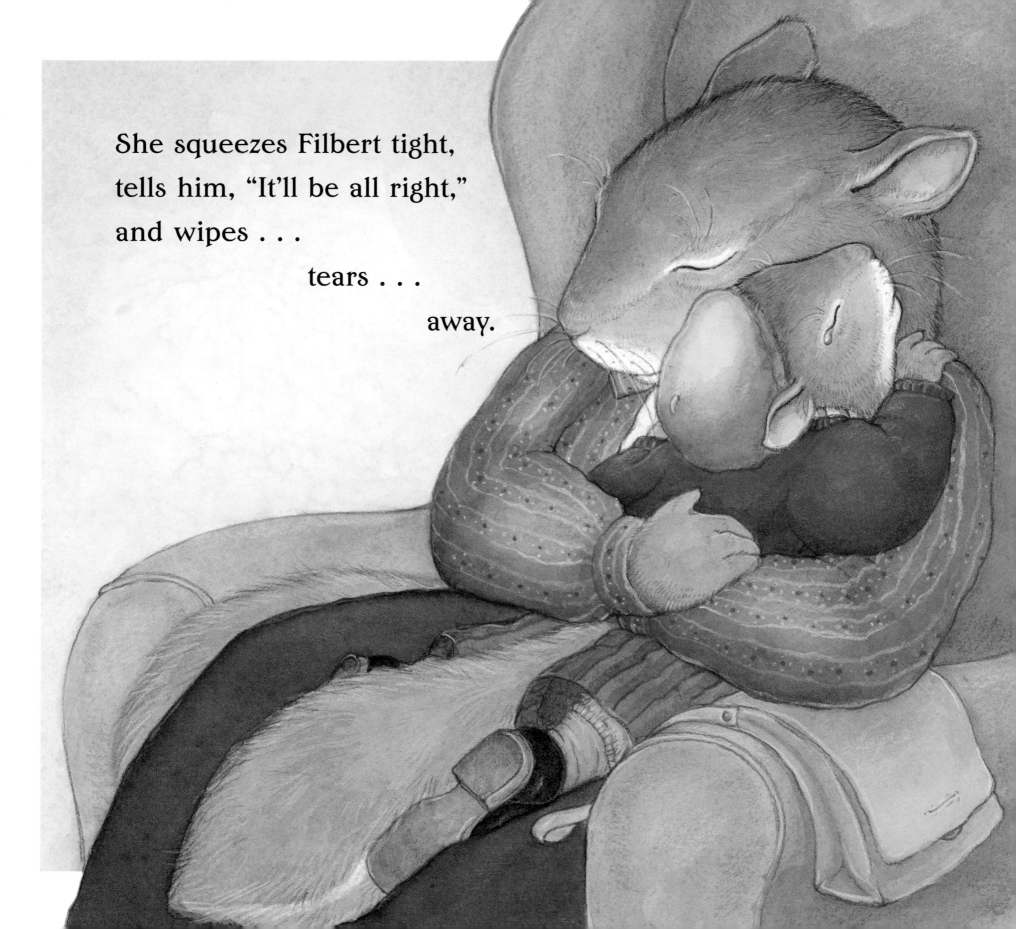

She squeezes Filbert tight,
tells him, "It'll be all right,"
and wipes . . .

tears . . .

away.

"I'll run back to Granny's!"
Filbert darts out the door

and leaps through the lot
as the soccer ball soars.

Swoosh! down the sideline.
Swish! swirls the breeze.

Goal! through the neighbor's butternut trees.

From the hollow of the oak,
Mama hopes and prays
and smiles when Filbert stops

to look . . .

both . . .

ways.